# BOYZ R

# Camping Out

Felice Arena and Phil Kettle

illustrated by
David Cox

MACMILLAN

First published 2003 by
MACMILLAN EDUCATION AUSTRALIA PTY LTD
15–19 Claremont Street, South Yarra 3141
Reprinted 2003, 2004, 2005, 2006, 2007 (twice), 2008, 2009

Visit our website at www.macmillan.com.au or
go directly to www.macmillanlibrary.com.au

Associated companies and representatives throughout the world.

Copyright © Felice Arena and Phil Kettle 2003

All rights reserved.
Except under the conditions described in the *Copyright Act 1968* of Australia
and subsequent amendments, no part of this publication may be reproduced,
stored in a retrieval system, or transmitted in any form or by any means,
electronic, mechanical, photocopying, recording or otherwise, without the
prior written permission of the copyright owner.

National Library of Australia
Cataloguing-in-Publication data

Arena, Felice.
  Camping out.

  For primary school children.
  ISBN 978 0 7329 8958 3.
  ISBN 978 0 7329 9178 4 (Set 1).

  1. Camping – Juvenile literature. I. Kettle, Phil. II.
  Title. (Series: Arena, Felice. Boyz rule).

A823.3

Project management by Limelight Press Pty Ltd
Cover and text design by Lore Foye
Illustrations by David Cox

Printed in Hong Kong

# Contents

*Josh*                    *Con*

# CHAPTER 1

# **Tent Tactics**

Con has invited his best friend Josh
to sleep over at his house. They
decide to experience the thrill of
camping in the great outdoors by
spending the entire night in a tent—
pitched in Con's backyard.

**Josh** "What if your backyard was the Serengeti plains in Africa, we probably wouldn't make it through the night."

**Con** "Why?"

**Josh** "Because we'd be eaten alive by lions. They'd rip through this tent in a second and tear us to bits. They'd go for our necks, then our guts—sucking out all the blood and air."

**Con** "Sick!"

**Josh** "They do a lot of their hunting at night—I saw it on TV once. There was this scene where they attacked all these sleeping elephants—it was so cool."

**Con** "Not for the elephants. Besides, if we were really camping in Africa we wouldn't pitch our tent where lions hang out."

**Josh** "Yeah, I know. I'm just saying, that's all."

**Con** "Phwoh!! Did you just let one off? It *stinks*! Like rotten eggs."

**Josh** (laughing) "It was a quiet one. I thought you wouldn't smell it."

**Con** "*Wouldn't smell it?* We're in a tent! It's silent, but deadly— a real SBD."

The boys chuckle and spend the
next few minutes telling each other
farting jokes. Eventually they decide
to get some sleep. A few moments
later, Josh jumps up out of his
sleeping bag and flicks on his torch.

**Josh** "Did you hear that? Are you awake?"

**Con** (groggy) "What? Hmm? Yeah, now I am! What's up?"

**Josh** "I heard something."

**Con** "What? Lions?"

**Josh** "No, I'm not joking! It sounded
like someone stepping on a stick."

**Con** "We don't have any sticks in
my backyard. Maybe you were
dreaming it."

**Josh** "Nah, it was real. Something
or someone's out there!"

**Con** "No they're not! Get back to
sleep."

Josh reluctantly flicks off the torch. But it isn't long before he springs up again out of his sleeping bag. This time, he sees that Con is also sitting upright.

**Josh** "*Now* did you hear that?"

**Con** "Yeah, I did!"

**Josh** "It could be an escaped
prisoner who's looking for
a hide-out."

**Con** "Yeah, right—in my backyard.
Maybe I should have a look?"

**Josh** "No!"

**Con** "Why?"

**Josh** "Because if it is a prisoner he won't want to get caught and he might do something terrible to you. He could be really dangerous!"

**Con** "The only thing that's
dangerous are your smelly farts—
man, that's off! Stop doing them.
I'm choking in here."

**Josh** "Sorry—I'm a bit nervous."

Once again, the boys suddenly hear the sound of sticks snapping— they both jump with fright.

**Josh** "Oh no, he's coming to get us!"
**Con** "Shhh! Stop freaking out. You're scaring me."
**Josh** (whispering) "Sorry. But if it's not an escaped prisoner, what do you think it is?"

**Con**  "I don't know."

**Josh**  "Could be an alien?"

**Con**  "You watch too much TV!"

**Josh**  "Well it could be! Aliens come down to Earth and take people all the time. Especially if you're out in the open like we are. They can probably see us right now from their spaceship."

**Con** "You mean they can probably *smell* us—stop farting will ya!"

Suddenly a shadow from out of nowhere appears standing at the entrance of the tent.

The boys scream.

**Con and Josh**

"AAAAARRRRRRGHHHHHH!!!!!!!!!!"

# CHAPTER 2

# **Phew!**

It's only Con's dad. He tells the boys
to go to sleep because he can hear
them from inside the house. He
leaves them and goes back to bed.

**Josh** "Phew! Lucky it was just your old man."

**Con** "Aliens and escaped prisoners—huh! You crack me up!"

**Josh** "Well, you were scared, too—admit it."

**Con** "Yeah, but not as much as you."

**Josh** "I'm hungry."

**Con** "Yeah so am I—there's some cake in the fridge."

**Josh** "Yeah!"

**Con** "Let's go—but be quiet. I don't want to wake anyone up."

The boys leave the tent and tiptoe
across the damp backyard lawn over
to the back door of Con's house.

**Con**  "Oh no! Dad's locked us out."

Con and Josh quietly wander
around the house trying every door.

**Con** "I can't believe this. We're totally locked out. We'll have to climb through a window. Look, my sister's window's open. Shhhh! Be really quiet. We can't wake her up or we'll be in big trouble."

**Josh** (whispering) "This is so cool. I feel like some secret commando breaking in to catch some bad guys."

**Con** "You really *do* watch too much TV!"

The boys climb really quietly in through Con's sister's bedroom window and carefully sneak across the room. Just then, Josh uncontrollably breaks wind—a loud, thunderous one that suddenly wakes up Con's sister. She screams as she sees the shadows of Con and Josh standing in front of her.

# CHAPTER 3

# Mystery Sound

Con's father and mother rush into
the room. They are not impressed to
see Con and Josh—even though the
boys try to explain how they were
hungry and locked out. After getting
a lecture and something to eat, Con
and Josh go back out to the tent.

**Con** "I think you need to see a fart
doctor or something!"

**Josh** "I didn't think it was gonna be
that loud. I thought I could
squeeze out another SBD. Sorry."

**Con** "Doesn't matter. I'm going to sleep now. Goodnight."

**Josh** "G'night."

A few minutes later, directly outside the boys' tent, there is a sudden sound of sticks snapping— again! The boys jump up out of their sleeping bags and flick the torch on.

**Josh** "Is that your dad again?
Please tell me it's your dad!"

**Con** "I don't think so."

**Josh** "See! I was right, the aliens
are back."

**Con** "Well whatever it is—I'm gonna
look."

**Josh** "I'm coming with ya!"

The boys unzip the tent and nervously stick their heads outside. They shine their torch frantically across the backyard, but nothing's there. Suddenly, the stick snapping sound starts up again.

Both boys gasp! They direct the
torch up into the trees at the edge of
the backyard, to discover the mystery
of the creepy sound—a possum
happily chewing and gnawing on
some branches.

**Josh** "A possum! That's it? A harmless possum!"

**Con** (chuckling) "I don't know about harmless. Maybe it's an alien possum or a possum that's escaped from a possum prison or ..."

**Josh** "Yeah, yeah, really funny."

The boys pop their heads back inside the tent and finally get to sleep. The only sounds heard for the rest of the evening are crickets chirping, sticks snapping and ... oh yes, Josh farting.

Josh

# BOYZ RULE!
# Camping Lingo

Con

**air bed**  A mattress that you blow up with a pump. An air bed is really comfortable to sleep on.

**compass**  A compass shows you where north, south, east and west are.

**cooler**  You put your food in a cooler to keep your food fresh. Another name is an esky. It's a good idea to take a cooler when you go camping.

**torch**  A torch is a light you can carry. It's really important to take a torch with you when you go camping.

33

# BOYZ RULE!

# Camping Must-dos

☞ Make sure you don't pitch your tent on an ant hill.

☞ Don't forget to take the insect repellent.

☞ Take plenty of food.

☞ Make sure that you put your campfire out before you go to sleep.

☞ Tell ghost stories before you go to sleep—it might scare away the creepy-crawlies!

☞ Make sure that your friend doesn't snore.

☞ If you camp in the backyard, make sure your parents don't lock the door. You might want to go inside in the middle of the night.

☞ If you are camping out near a river, make sure you don't sleepwalk—you might get wet!

☞ If you have a dog, let him sleep in the tent with you. Dogs are good at scaring wild animals away.

☞ The most important thing to remember to take camping is toilet paper, and a spade to bury it!

☞ Wear old clothes—your good clothes might get wrecked.

# BOYZ RULE!

## Camping
## Instant Info

 One of the largest tents ever was made in 1952 and measured 28.1 metres by 14.6 metres.

 Scouts spend a lot of time camping. The Boy Scout movement was formed by Robert Baden-Powell in England.

 Campers learn to tell the best bedtime scary stories.

 Possums come out at night because they are nocturnal creatures.

People go camping all over the world in tents of all shapes and sizes.

 The most common type of tent is a two-person tent.

# BOYZ RULE!
# Think Tank

1 What should you do with your campfire before you go to sleep?

2 What is a teepee?

3 What do you do if the person who's sleeping in your tent snores?

4 Where do you go to the toilet when you are camping in the bush?

5 What should you do with your rubbish when you leave the campsite?

6 What is the best food to eat when you go camping?

7 What do you do if a wild animal comes into your tent?

8 What do mosquitoes like to eat most of all?

# Answers

**1** Always put your campfire out … always.

**2** A teepee is a tent Native Americans use.

**3** If someone in your tent snores, put in earplugs or tell them to sleep outside.

**4** You go to the toilet behind a big tree when you are camping out.

**5** Never leave your rubbish—always take it with you.

**6** Baked beans are the best food to eat when you are camping.

**7** If a wild animal comes into your tent, scream or pretend to be asleep … and hope that it goes away.

**8** Mosquitoes like to eat your blood most of all.

# How did you score?

- If you got all 8 answers right then you can pack your tent and go camping.

- If you got only 4 answers correct pitch your tent in the backyard.

- If you got fewer than 4 answers correct you'd better stay home … inside!

39

Felice → ← Phil

Hi Guys!

We have heaps of fun reading and want you to, too. We both believe that being a good reader is really important and so cool.

Try out our suggestions to help you have fun as you read.

At school, why don't you use "Camping Out" as a play and you and your friends can be the actors. Set the scene for your play. Use your imagination and pretend that you are at your favourite camping spot. It is just starting to get dark.

So ... have you decided who is going to be Josh and who is going to be Con? Now, with your friends, read and act out our story in front of the class.

We have a lot of fun when we go to schools and read our stories. After we finish the kids all clap really loudly. When you've finished your play your classmates will do the same. Just remember to look out the window—there might be a talent scout from a television station watching you!

Reading at home is really important and a lot of fun as well.

Take our books home and get someone in your family to read them with you. Maybe they can take on a part in the story.

Remember, reading is a whole lot of fun.

So, as the frog in the local pond would say, Read-it!

And remember, Boyz Rule!

# When We Were Kids

*Felice*

*Phil*

**Felice** "Did you ever worry about wild creatures when you camped as a kid?"

**Phil** "Yeah, I remember once I was attacked while I was asleep in my tent."

**Felice** "Really? That's terrible!"

**Phil** "These creatures were really hungry for my blood."

**Felice** "That's shocking. And you survived."

**Phil** "Yeah, but only just."

**Felice** "So what were these vicious creatures?"

**Phil** "Some people call them cannibals, but I call them mosquitoes!"

# BOYZ RULE!

# What a Laugh!

**Q** What did the mosquito say the first time it saw a camel's hump?

**A** Did I do that?

# *BOYZ RULE!*

Read about the fun that boys have in these ***BOYZ RULE!*** titles:

**Park Soccer**

**Golf Legends**

**Yabby Hunt**

**The Tree House**

**Bike Daredevils**

**Camping Out**

**Gone Fishing**

**Water Rats**

**and more ... !**